# ON THE DAY
# PETER STUYVESANT
# SAILED INTO TOWN

by ARNOLD LOBEL

A Harper Trophy Book
HARPER & ROW, PUBLISHERS

ON THE DAY PETER STUYVESANT SAILED INTO TOWN
Copyright © 1971 by Arnold Lobel

All rights reserved. No part of this book may be used or reproduced in
any manner whatsoever without written permission except in the case
of brief quotations embodied in critical articles and reviews. Printed in
the United States of America. For information address Harper & Row,
Publishers, Inc., 10 East 53rd St., New York, N.Y. 10022. Published
simultaneously in Canada by Fitzhenry & Whiteside Limited, Toronto.
Library of Congress Catalog Card Number: 75-148420
ISBN 0-06-023971-9
ISBN 0-06-023972-7 (lib. bdg.)
ISBN 0-06-443144-4 (pbk.)
First Harper Trophy edition, 1987.

for Adelaide Oppenheim

## ABOUT PETER STUYVESANT

*Peter Stuyvesant came to America in the spring of 1647. He had been appointed Director-General for the Dutch colony of New Netherland. Most of the population in the colony was centered in New Amsterdam, a village located at the tip of Manhattan Island. The first families settled on the island in 1624. They were sent there by the Dutch West India Company to set up a fur-trading post for European markets.*

*Stuyvesant found that his new community had serious troubles. Severe weather, repeated attacks from Indian tribes, and the poor leadership of two governors before him had brought New Amsterdam to near collapse. The streets of the town were weed-covered and dirty; and animals ran about freely, eating the garbage that lay everywhere. Houses were made of timber with thatched roofs; they burned down frequently. And the walls of the town fort were crumbling.*

*Stuyvesant, to put it mildly, was not an even-tempered man. He was outraged at what he saw and quickly set forth a series of proclamations and laws to improve life within the settlement.*

*Under Peter Stuyvesant, the next decade was a time of great progress for New Amsterdam. By 1660, its population had doubled, trade prospered, and in appearance the town could rival Dutch communities in Europe. Peter Stuyvesant's stern control had seen the colony through its crisis, and New Netherland became a pleasant place in which to live.*

*Arnold Lobel*

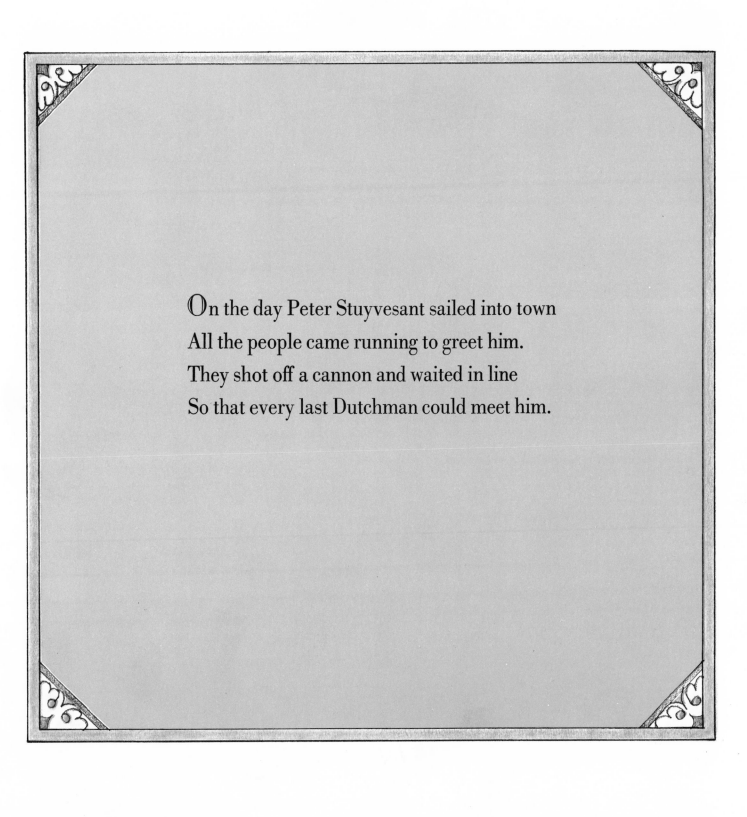

On the day Peter Stuyvesant sailed into town
All the people came running to greet him.
They shot off a cannon and waited in line
So that every last Dutchman could meet him.

"My friends," Peter said, "it is nice to be here
For my voyage was really a long one.
I will rule this new land with a very firm hand,
And my government will be a strong one.
Yes, my government will be a strong one."

Peter Stuyvesant stood with a leg made of wood,
And he said, "There is no time to talk now.
It's a very fine day, this eleventh of May,
So I think I will go for a walk now."

And into New Amsterdam Peter did go

To see all there was to be seen.

But he soon wore a frown as he walked up and down—

He discovered that nothing was clean.

The governor slipped in the mud and the mire,

And he said, "Things are not at all well here.

I am standing in garbage right up to my knees,

And the air has a very bad smell here.

Yes, the air has a very bad smell here."

"All the houses in town are in need of repair,"
Peter shouted. "I loudly decry it!
This whole dirty place is a total disgrace.
Good Dutchmen, we must beautify it!"

But the folk of the town went on smoking their pipes,
And they said, "It is best to ignore him.
There will soon come a day he will be on his way
Like the men who have governed before him."

From Broadway to Wall Street old Stuyvesant stormed;
With a tap and a step he kept walking,
While some chickens and ducks made a nest in his hat
And some geese on the path made a squawking.
Yes, those geese on the path made a squawking.

Then a goat from behind, in a manner unkind,
Gave Peter a push on his seat.
A cow licked his nose and some pigs chewed his toes
As poor Stuyvesant sat in the street.

"This New World is a mess!" Peter cried in distress.
"These animals need gates and fences.
Take these birds to a cage!" Peter shouted in rage.
"Oh, good Dutchmen, let's come to our senses!"

As his voice rocked the ground with a great, booming sound,

Like a sky filled with thunder and lightning,

Those good Dutchmen did shake—they cried, "Make no mistake,

This man's temper is really quite frightening!"

While the citizens stood in a trembling group

Peter cried, "Here is my proclamation.

All you men and you maids, get your brooms and your spades.

We must work now without hesitation!

Yes, let's work now without hesitation!"

So they put up new buildings all sturdy and strong,

And they cleaned all the rubbish away.

They mended the fences and paved many streets

From the top of the town to the bay.

They filled up the holes in the walls of the fort,
For the colony needed protection.
And the people agreed they were clever to heed
Peter Stuyvesant's careful direction.

Some ten or twelve summers had come and had gone
As they worked on the east and the west side.
Things were going so well it was soon hard to tell
Which half of that town was the best side.

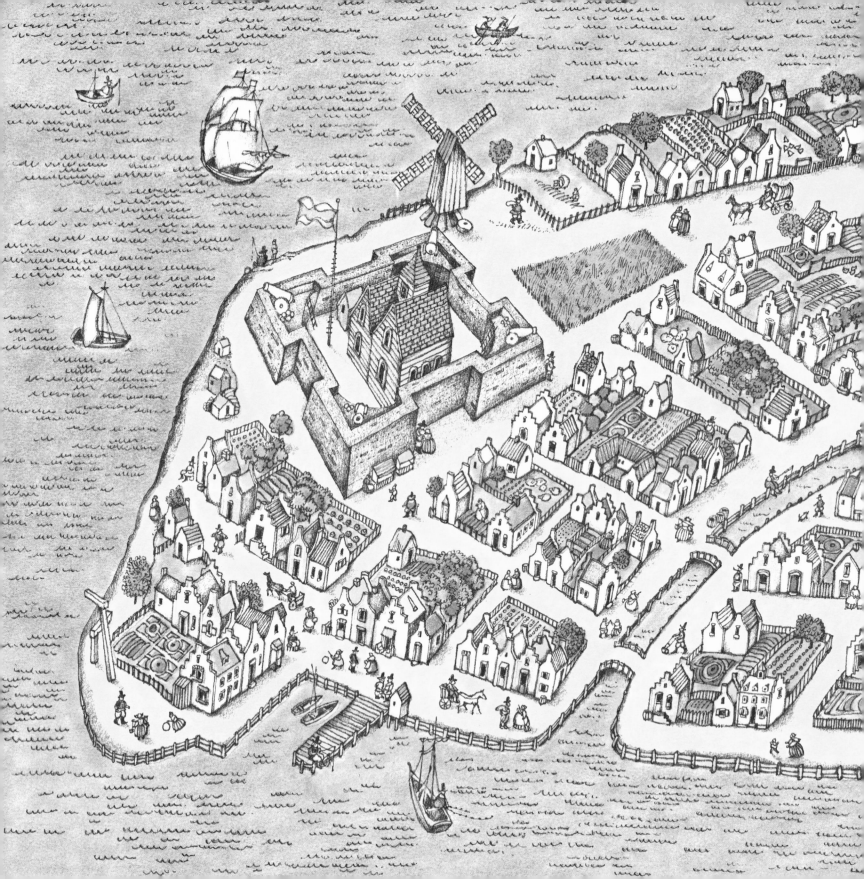

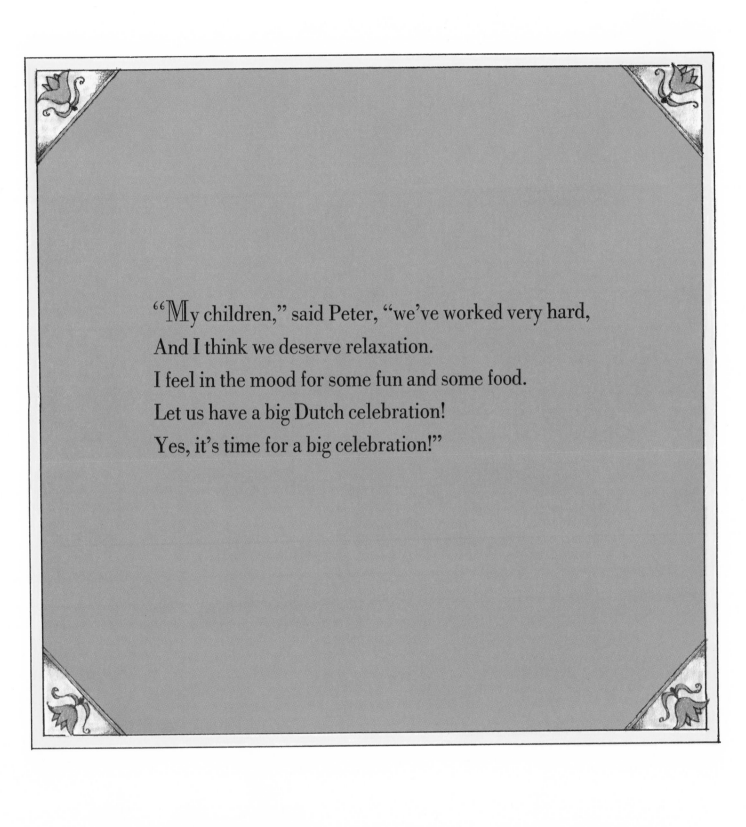

"My children," said Peter, "we've worked very hard,
And I think we deserve relaxation.
I feel in the mood for some fun and some food.
Let us have a big Dutch celebration!
Yes, it's time for a big celebration!"

Each New Amsterdam nose sniffed the smells that arose
In delicious fat clouds to the air.
How they gave such delight to each Dutch appetite,
All those good things to eat everywhere.

Someone asked, "Will this town stay as small as it is?"

Well, of course, there was no way of knowing,

So they danced until evening all dizzy and gay

And went home as the darkness was growing.

That night Peter Stuyvesant heard a strange sound

Underneath a round moon brightly gleaming.

It swept past his door, a great tumble and roar,

But old Stuyvesant knew he was dreaming . . .

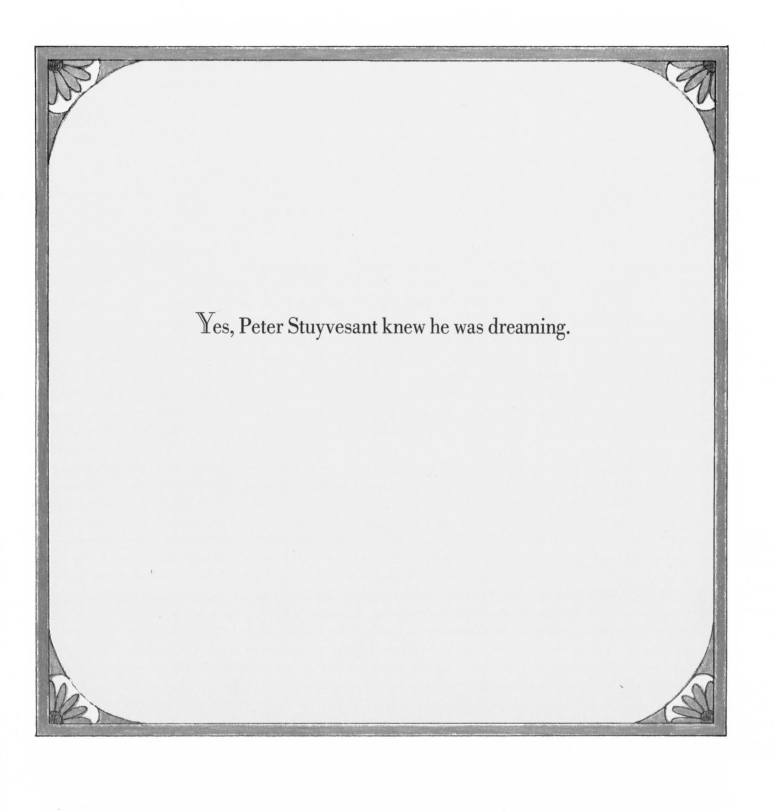

Yes, Peter Stuyvesant knew he was dreaming.